Autumn Festival Fun

adapted by Tina Gallo

Ready-to-Read

Simon Spotlight

New York   London   Toronto   Sydney   New Delhi

SIMON SPOTLIGHT

An imprint of Simon & Schuster Children's Publishing Division

1230 Avenue of the Americas, New York, New York 10020

This Simon Spotlight paperback edition September 2017

For information about special discounts for bulk purchases, please contact Simon & Schuster Special Sales at
1-866-506-1949 or business@simonandschuster.com.

Manufactured in the United States of America 0817 LAK

2 4 6 8 10 9 7 5 3 1

ISBN 978-1-5344-0189-1 (hc)

ISBN 978-1-5344-0188-4 (pbk)

ISBN 978-1-5344-0190-7 (eBook)

Po went to the noodle shop
to talk to his dad, Mr. Ping.

Mr. Ping was happy to see Po. "Po! There you are!" he exclaimed. "The Autumn Festival is in a week, and we need to bake moon cakes!"

"I know, Dad. But I'm too busy to help this year," Po said. "What could be more important than helping your father bake 2,700 moon cakes?" Mr. Ping asked.

"Hmm. Maybe being responsible for the safety of all who reside in the Valley of Peace?" Po replied. But the next day Mr. Ping caught Po acting silly with Monkey.

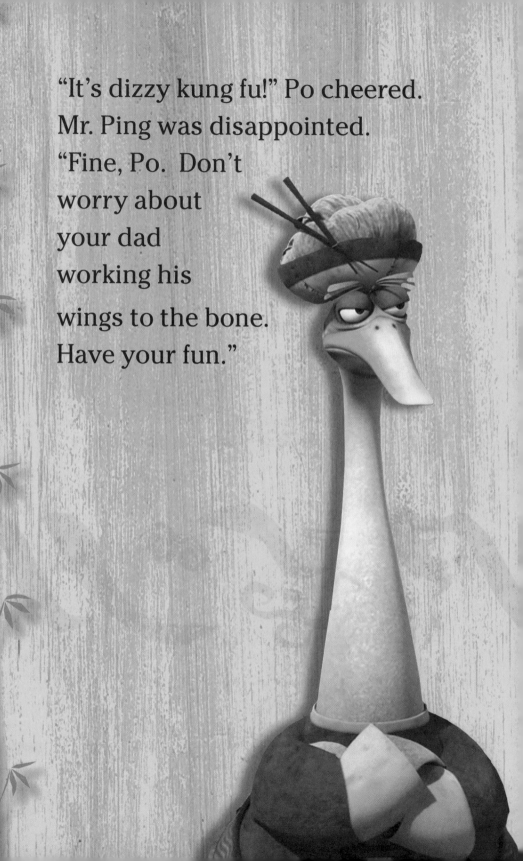

"It's dizzy kung fu!" Po cheered.
Mr. Ping was disappointed.
"Fine, Po. Don't
worry about
your dad
working his
wings to the bone.
Have your fun."

"I think Dad has gotten lonely
since I moved out,"
Po said to Monkey.
"Get him something to keep him
company," Monkey suggested.
"Like a plant."

"That's it!" Po shouted.
"You're getting him a plant?"
Monkey asked.
"No, a girlfriend," Po replied.

Po visited his dad the next day.
"I thought you could use
a little company," Po said.
"I got you a date!"
He was excited for his dad
to have dinner with Mrs. Yoon.

Po served the couple their meal.
"Look! A romantic dinner—two
servings of soup in one large bowl,"
Po said.
Mrs. Yoon smiled at Mr. Ping.
"I made us some nice steamed buns
for the occasion."

"What? You dare to ruin
the purity of my noodles
with these buns? Get out!"
Mr. Ping yelled.
Mrs. Yoon left, a little confused.
"I had a lovely time," she said.

Po didn't understand why
his father was being so rude.
"Dad, what's going on?" Po asked.
"All right. I'll let you in on my
secret," Mr. Ping said.
"I already have a girlfriend."

"What? Really? That's great!" Po said. Suddenly, he noticed Scorpion was in the noodle shop. "Dad, look out! Scorpion's back to seek her revenge!" Po yelled.

"No, Po, you don't understand," Mr. Ping said. "Scorpion is my girlfriend." Po gasped.

"She must have brainwashed you with her Scorpion poison," Po said.
"Oh, Po. I'm not evil anymore," Scorpion said sweetly.
"What changed you?" Po asked.

"The love of a good goose,"
Scorpion said.
"Isn't she beautiful?" Mr. Ping
said dreamily. "Look at all
those gorgeous eyes."

Po decided to give Scorpion a
chance.
He went back to the noodle shop the
next day. Scorpion was there alone.
"I thought we could make
moon cakes together," Po told her.
"How sweet!" Scorpion said.

Po was wearing the Autumn Festival
clown costume to make
Mr. Ping happy.
Scorpion offered Po a moon cake.
"These are seriously good," Po said.
"I won a baking contest because
I brainwashed the judges,"
Scorpion said.

Po laughed. "I thought you were going to brainwash my dad."

"That's silly," Scorpion replied. "Why would I do that when I could poison everyone in the Valley?"

"What?" Po cried.
"That's right," Scorpion said.
"In fact, I'm poisoning you
right now. It won't kill you,
but it will make you defenseless."

"I was right not to trust you,"
Po said. He was dizzy and his
words were getting slurred.
It was difficult to talk.
Scorpion laughed wickedly.

Mr. Ping arrived back at the
noodle shop.
"Hi, honey. Po stopped by and left
you a message," Scorpion said.
"He said he never wants to see
your face again."

Mr. Ping was shocked.

"He said that?" he asked.

"Yes," Scorpion said sweetly.
From the back room Po tried
desperately to talk.

"Noooooo," he slurred.

"Did you hear that?" Mr. Ping said.
"It's probably the neighbors,"
Scorpion said.
"Come on. The festival awaits.
If Po really loves you, he'll
find you there."

When Scorpion and Mr. Ping
arrived at the festival,
Master Shifu was just starting
his opening speech.

"Everyone, please grab a moon cake for my ceremonial speech, followed by the ceremonial eating of the moon cakes, followed by the ceremonial ceremony."

Master Shifu raised a moon cake.
"Don't . . . eat . . . that!" Po slurred.
Tigress took a bite of moon cake.
Suddenly, she felt dizzy.
"What's going on?" she said,
then she passed out.

Everyone who ate a moon cake
passed out.
But Scorpion was shocked when
Po was suddenly at her side.
"You can fight me?" she gasped.
"How?"

"Dizzy kung fu," Po explained.
"I made it up myself."
Po was able to defeat Scorpion.
Later on, Mr. Ping and
Po were cooking noodles
together.

"What's more fun than making 2,700 noodles to combat Scorpion's poison?" Mr. Ping said.

"Po grinned. "Hey, Dad, look!
You have some lady admirers
over there."
Po expected Mr. Ping to say he
wasn't interested.
But he just gave a sly smile!